Copyright © 2011 by NordSüd Verlag AG, CH-8005 Zürich, Switzerland.
First published in Switzerland under the title *Die chinesische Nachtigall*.
English text copyright © 2011 by North-South Books Inc., New York 10001.
English adaptation by Pirkko Vainio. Edited by Susan Pearson.
All rights reserved.
No part of this book may be reproduced or utilized in any form or by any means, electronic or
mechanical, including photo-copying, recording, or any information storage and retrieval system,
without permission in writing from the publisher.

First published in the United States, Great Britain, Canada, Australia, and New Zealand in 2011
by North-South Books Inc., an imprint of NordSüd Verlag AG, CH-8005 Zürich, Switzerland.
Distributed in the United States by North-South Books Inc., New York 10001.

Library of Congress Cataloging-in-Publication Data is available.
Printed in Germany by Grafisches Centrum Cuno GmbH & Co. KG, 39240 Calbe, April 2011.
ISBN: 978-0-7358-4029-4 (trade edition)
1 3 5 7 9 • 10 8 6 4 2

www.northsouth.com

FSC
www.fsc.org
MIX
Paper from
responsible sources
FSC® C043106

The
NIGHTINGALE

BY HANS CHRISTIAN ANDERSEN · ILLUSTRATED BY PIRKKO VAINIO

NorthSouth
New York / London

This story happened long, long ago; but that is all the more reason for telling it again, lest it be forgotten.

In China there lived an Emperor whose palace was the most splendid in all the world. In the palace gardens were the most wonderful flowers, and tied to the most beautiful were silver bells that tinkled so that no one should pass by without noticing them. The garden was so big that not even the gardener himself knew where it ended, and everything in it was perfectly planned.

If you kept walking, you came to a beautiful forest with tall trees and deep lakes. The woods went on until they reached the sea, which was deep enough for great ships to sail right under the branches of the trees. In these branches lived a nightingale that sang so beautifully that even a poor fisherman casting his nets at night stopped still to listen.

Travelers from all around the world came to the Emperor's city, and they admired everything very much, especially the palace and the gardens. But when they heard the nightingale, they all said, "This is better than anything." And they went home and told everyone about the nightingale. Learned scholars wrote many books about the city and the palace and the gardens, and no one forgot about the nightingale—it was always praised over everything else.

Those books were read all over the world, and in the course of time some of them reached the Emperor. He sat in his golden chair and read and read, frequently nodding his head, pleased with the delightful descriptions of his city, his palace, and his gardens. "But the nightingale is the best of all," he read.

"What's this?" exclaimed the Emperor. "The nightingale? I know nothing about a nightingale! Is it possible that there is such a bird in my empire—even in my garden—and I have never heard of it?" And he sent for his chamberlain.

"There is said to be a wonderful bird in my garden called a nightingale!" said the Emperor.

"I have never heard anyone mention it," replied the Chamberlain.

"I wish it to appear this evening and sing for me," said the Emperor. "I cannot have the whole world knowing what I possess when I do not know it myself!"

"I will seek it, and I shall find it," said the Chamberlain.

But where was the bird to be found? The Chamberlain ran up and down the staircases, through the halls and passages with half of the court following him, but no one he asked had ever heard of the bird. At last they found a poor little kitchen maid who said, "Oh, yes, the nightingale! I know it well. It sings so beautifully that it brings tears to my eyes, for it feels just as if my mother kissed me!"

The little kitchen maid led the Chamberlain and half of the court to the forest where the nightingale usually sang, and as they were walking along, a cow began to moo.

"Oh!" cried the courtiers. "There it is! What a powerful voice from such a tiny creature!"

"No, that's the cow mooing," said the little kitchen maid. "We are still a long way from the place."

Now the frogs began to croak in the marsh.

"Glorious!" said the court chaplain. "It sounds just like little church bells."

"No, those are frogs!" said the little kitchen maid. "But I think we'll be hearing it soon now."

And then the nightingale began to sing.

"That's it," said the little kitchen maid. "Listen, listen. And there it sits." And she pointed to a little gray bird up in the branches.

"Is it possible?" cried the Chamberlain. "I should never have thought it looked so ordinary! It must have lost its color at seeing so many distinguished people around it."

"Little nightingale," called the kitchen maid. "Our gracious emperor wishes you to sing before him."

"With the greatest pleasure," replied the nightingale, and it began to sing joyfully.

"It sounds like crystal bells!" said the Chamberlain.

"That bird will be a great success at court. My excellent little nightingale, I have the honor of inviting you to a banquet this evening where you shall charm his Imperial Majesty with your beautiful singing."

"My song sounds best out here in the forest," replied the nightingale, but it went with them willingly when it heard that the Emperor wished it.

The palace had been decorated for the occasion. The porcelain walls and floor gleamed in the light of thousands of golden lamps. The most beautiful flowers had been placed in the hallways, and in all the hustle and bustle, all the bells began to ring. You could hardly hear yourself speak.

In the middle of the great hall, where the Emperor sat, a golden perch had been placed for the nightingale. The whole court was present, and the little kitchen maid had been permitted to stand behind the door, for now she had been given the title of Cook.

Everyone was looking at the little gray bird as the Emperor nodded for it to begin.

The nightingale sang so beautifully that tears filled the Emperor's eyes and rolled down his cheeks. Then the nightingale sang even more sweetly, and its song went straight to the Emperor's heart.

The Emperor was so pleased, he wanted to give the nightingale his golden slipper to wear around its neck. But the nightingale told him, "I have seen tears in the Emperor's eyes, and that is the richest treasure. I have been rewarded enough." And then it sang again in its sweet voice.

The Emperor decided that the nightingale must now remain at court. It was given its own cage and was allowed to go out twice each day and once each night. Twelve servants, each holding a silken ribbon fastened to the bird's leg, accompanied the nightingale when it went out. There was really no pleasure in that sort of an outing.

One day the Emperor received a package. On the outside of it the word *Nightingale* was written.

"Ah, it must be a new book about our famous bird," said the Emperor. But it was not a book. It was a little work of art lying in a box, a mechanical nightingale exactly like the living one except that it was decorated all over with diamonds, rubies, and sapphires. When it was wound up, it sang one of the pieces that the real bird sang and then its tail wagged up and down, glittering with silver and gold. Around its neck was a little ribbon on which was written *The Emperor of Japan's nightingale is poor compared to that of the Emperor of China's.*

"Beautiful!" everyone said, and the person who had brought the package immediately received the title of Imperial Nightingale Bringer.

"Now they must sing together—what a duet that will be!"

And so the birds had to sing together, but it did not go very well, for the real nightingale sang in its own way and the mechanical bird sang only in waltz time. But when it sang alone, the mechanical bird was just as successful as the real bird and much more beautiful as well. It sang the same melody thirty-three times without getting tired at all.

The people wanted to hear it again, but the Emperor said that the living nightingale should have a turn. But where was it?

No one had noticed that it had flown out the open window, back to its green forest.

The whole court agreed that the nightingale was a very ungrateful creature. "But we have the best bird," they said, and then the mechanical bird had to sing again.

The Imperial Music Master praised the bird extravagantly. "For you see, ladies and gentlemen, with a real nightingale you never know what song is coming next, but with this mechanical bird you always know what to expect. You can even open it up and show people where the waltzes come from."

The following Sunday the bird was shown to the public. "Everyone must hear it," the Emperor said. So the people heard the mechanical bird, and they were extremely pleased. They all said "Oooh!" and held up their forefingers and nodded.

But the poor fisherman who had heard the real nightingale said, "It sounds pretty enough, and it is very nearly like the real one, but there is something missing."

The real nightingale was banished from the empire, and the mechanical bird was placed on a silken cushion close to the Emperor's bed and given the title of Chief Imperial After-Dinner Singer.

A whole year passed. By then the Emperor, the court, and everyone in China knew the mechanical bird's song by heart, but they liked it all the better for now they could sing along.

But one evening when the mechanical bird was singing its best and the Emperor lay in bed listening to it, something inside the bird went "*Whizzz-whirrr-*POP!" and then the music stopped.

The Emperor sprang out of bed and called for his doctor, but what could *he* do? Then he sent for the watchmaker, who got the bird to work in some way; but he warned that it must be played only once a year, for its works were terribly worn.

Five years passed and a great sorrow came to the whole empire. The people really were fond of their emperor, and now he was ill and could not, it was said, live much longer.

Cold and pale, the Emperor lay on his gorgeous bed with its long velvet curtains and heavy gold tassels. High above him a window stood open, and the moon shone in on his face. The poor emperor could hardly breathe; he felt as if he had a weight on his chest. He opened his eyes and then he saw that Death himself was sitting on his chest and was wearing the Emperor's golden crown. In one hand he held the Emperor's sword and in the other his beautiful banner. And all around, in the folds of the velvet curtains, strange heads appeared. Some of them were ugly; others were lovely. These were all the Emperor's bad and good deeds standing before him, whispering, "Remember this? Remember that?"

"I don't remember!" cried the Emperor. "Music, music! So I don't have to hear what they are saying. Precious golden bird, sing, sing!"

But the bird remained silent. No one was there to wind it up.

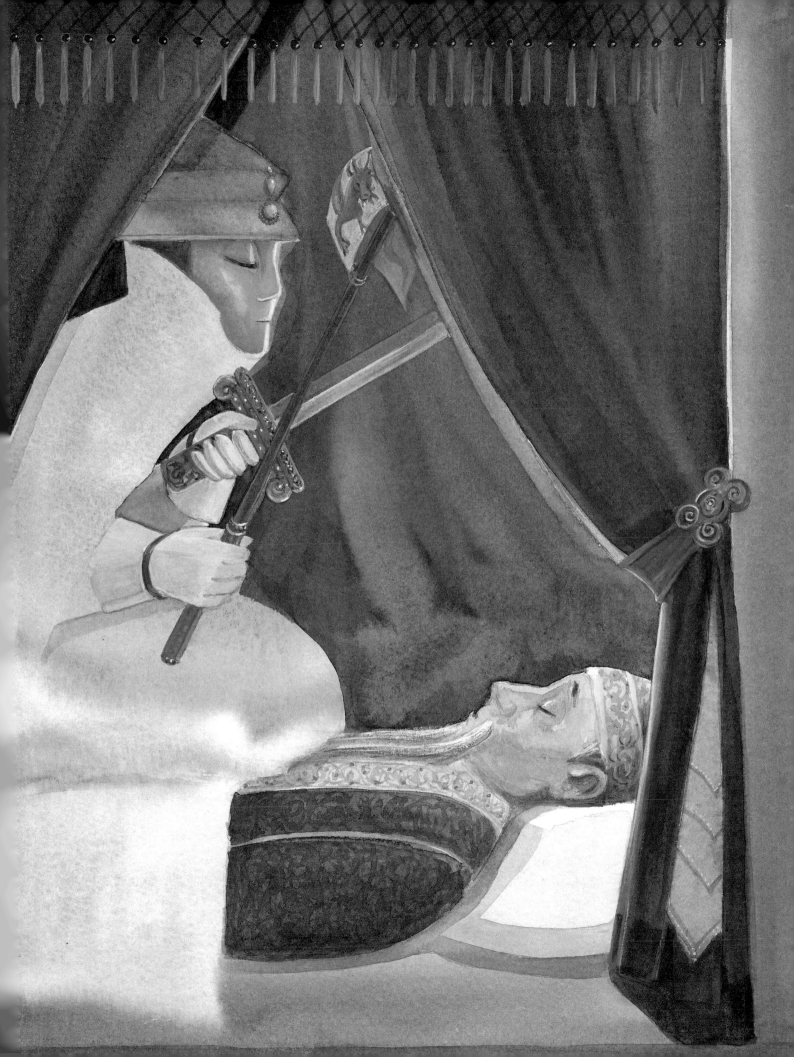

Suddenly the loveliest song came through the window. It was the little live nightingale, perched on a branch outside. It had heard of the Emperor's torments and had come to bring him comfort and hope. And as it sang, the strange faces around the Emperor's bed grew paler and paler, and the blood ran more quickly through the Emperor's weak limbs. Even Death himself listened and said, "Go on, little nightingale, go on!" Then Death felt a longing for his own garden, and he slipped away out the window like a cold, white mist.

"Thank you, thank you!" said the Emperor. "You heavenly little bird! I banished you from my empire, and still you came back to sing Death away with your song. How can I reward you?"

"You have already rewarded me," replied the nightingale. "I saw the tears in your eyes the first time I ever sang for you, and I will never forget that. But sleep now and grow fresh and strong again while I sing to you."

When the Emperor awoke, the sun was shining and he was strong and well. The nightingale was still there, singing.

"You must stay with me always!" said the Emperor.

"I cannot build my nest and live in this palace," said the nightingale, "but let me come when I please. Then I will sit on the branch by your window and sing to cheer you and to make you thoughtful. I will sing about those who are happy and those who suffer. I will sing about the good and evil hidden around you. A little songbird must fly far and wide—to the poor fisherman, to the peasant, to people who live far away from you and your court. But I love your heart more than your crown, and I will always return to you."

Then the nightingale flew away.

When the servants came in to look after their dead emperor, they found him standing there. And the Emperor said, "Good morning."